TEA & SYMPATHETIC MAGIC

TANSY RAYNER ROBERTS

ISBN: 978-0-648-76396-3 (ebook)

ISBN: 978-0-6487639-7-0 (paperback)

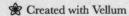 Created with Vellum

For Evelina, Elinor, Emma and Elizabeth

CONTENTS

DRAMATIS PERSONAE

Miss Mnemosyne "Mneme" Seabourne, an eligible lady

Mr Charles Thornbury, a spellcracker of note

Henry Jupiter, the Duke of Storm, an eligible Duke with a splendid library

Miss Letty Agnew, a friendly face

Lady Agnew, an accomplished hostess of garden parties

Mrs Galatea Seabourne, a matchmaking mamma, mistress of Shellwich Standing.

Antiope Seabourne, former Duchess of Storm (deceased)

Mrs Hecate Seabourne, a scheming mamma

DRAMATIS PERSONAE

MISS METIS SEABOURNE, A POOR RELATION

MRS JUNO VON TRASK, AN AMBITIOUS WIDOW

LADY LIESL OF SANDWICH, A RENOWNED BEAUTY

COLONEL WINTERBOURNE, AN UNTHREATENING
GENTLEMAN

DR SIMON ST SWITHINS, AN UNTHREATENING GENTLEMAN
DOCTOR

LADY EUROPA LOVAGE, A HIRED HOSTESS WITH MANY
DAUGHTERS

MRS PAULA DAZE, A LADY NOVELIST AND HIRED
CHAPERONE

SADIE, A HELPFUL MAID WITH MANY SISTERS

QUEEN AUD, DOES NOT APPEAR IN THIS STORY

ALFRED LORD MANTICORE, ALSO DOES NOT APPEAR IN
THIS STORY

MR SEABOURNE, A QUIET AND RETIRING PAPA WITH GREAT
FAITH IN HIS DAUGHTER AND A TASTE FOR THE ISLE OF
BATH, DOES NOT APPEAR IN THIS STORY

A PRIESTESS

DIVERSE SERVANTS AND GUESTS

CHAPTER 1

*I*f anyone had told Miss Mnemosyne Seabourne (Mneme for short) that she should grow up to be the sort of person who was bored of garden parties, she would have declared then and there that growing up was off the table.

Little Mneme had been an outspoken child, to the constant frustration of her mamma, and adored parties because cakes and conversation were her favourite things. She dreamed of a future when she was Out in Society, attending croquet games and glamorous balls, ready to catch a dazzling husband.

These days, at twenty-two years old, she would much rather be at home in her father's library, with a cup of tea and a book. There was, as it turned out, a ceiling on how many garden parties you could attend before they all became dismally dull.

Lady Agnew's garden party was the fourteenth Mneme had attended since this Season (her fifth since coming Out) began, and she was about ready to throw a teacup at the next person who informed her that it was a lovely day.

It *was* a lovely day. The sunshine was perfect. The roses were in bloom. The cakes were frosted in charming shades of blush pink and cornflower blue. There was the promise of sweetened ices later, and an eligible Duke on the premises.

Everything was awful.

"Is your tea to your liking?" asked Miss Letty Agnew, daughter of today's hostess. Only on her first Season, she had not yet been crushed flat by the disappointments of the marriage market.

Mneme smiled as genuinely as she dared. Most of her energies these days were poured into appearing dull; today that meant blending into the crowd of lovely, eligible young ladies in muslin frocks who danced attendance upon His Grace. "My tea is perfect," she said, keeping a careful eye upon the man of the hour, who stood in the centre of the pungent chamomile lawn in his bright orange cravat (which clashed with his even brighter beard), laughing loudly at something.

"We source the blend from a darling little plantation on the Isle of Dormouse," said the very young Miss Agnew, her voice trailing off as she realised that her audience was less than enthusiastic for the topic. "Oh. You're not interested in tea."

"I am very interested in tea," Mneme assured her. "Tea is the centre of my thoughts. I have drunk three cups this afternoon already, each more splendid than the last."

Tea rarely disappointed her. Tea would never ruin her chances at a decent marriage by constantly hurling her at the highest-ranked and least appropriate suitors, refusing to listen to a word she said about what she actually wanted...

It was possible that tea was no longer entirely the centre of her thoughts.

Across the lawn, Henry Jupiter, the Duke of Storm,

2

laughed at something one of his admirers said. His entire body shook as he indulged in a guffaw far longer and louder than society deemed polite. A lightning bolt of power sizzled in the air above his head, and no one batted an eye at that either because a Duke was allowed to be as rude or careless as he liked. Everyone of a lower rank was expected to keep their magical abilities buttoned up and quiet, when there was tea to be sipped and polite conversation to be made.

The Duke of Storm's entire existence was infuriating to Mneme. He held out an empty teacup as if expecting it to be snatched by empty air — and oh, there was one of his three personal footmen, who did indeed replace the empty cup with a brimming one, without the Duke having to wait more than a second or two.

The universe was infuriating, that such rituals existed to meet the exact needs of men who had done nothing to deserve them.

Henry wasn't even a particularly terrible example of a Duke; but because he *was* a Duke, no one would ever demand that he improve his character to any degree. At least when his mother the late Duchess was alive, there was someone who brooked none of his nonsense.

Mneme's teacup rattled in her saucer. She caught Miss Agnew staring in alarm at her too-firm grip on the delicate handle, and corrected the hold so that the teacup was less in danger of being snapped to pieces. "I wish he'd choose a wife already," Mneme huffed. "Then some of us could breathe out for the rest of the Season."

"I wish he'd choose me," Miss Agnew blurted, and blushed.

"Be careful what you wish for," said Mneme automatically, a ritual phrase often spoken in magical households. She caught sight of her mamma, fluttering around the

3

Duke of Storm like a hungry butterfly, and turned away with a sigh. "Marrying a Duke is *not* all it's cracked up to be."

"But he's so almost handsome, and he does cut a fine figure in his suits," Miss Agnew protested. "The Queen often invites him to advise her of matters of state, which means his wife will surely be invited to several royal events every year, and so many parties. Also, they say the ducal estate of Storm has the finest library in all the Isles. Three thousand volumes!"

"A fine library does increase the appeal of any potential husband," Mneme conceded. She thought better of Miss Agnew, that she counted the library as a bonus to a gentleman's appeal. "If only one could be sure that he had ever read a book."

"Oh dear," said Miss Agnew in despair as her own mother Lady Agnew took the arm of the Duke, whisking him along the lawn. A parade of whirling muslin dresses fell in behind them, none of his admirers wishing to be left behind. "I do believe it's time for croquet."

"Balls," said Mneme, and then grinned impishly at Miss Agnew, who spluttered out a very unladylike laugh in return. "Very well," she said, with a sigh to show that it was a great inconvenience. "I suppose we can be friends despite your terrible taste in suitors."

"He's not my suitor," said Miss Agnew, her blush reaching higher on her cheeks. "I've only been introduced to him twice."

"Mnemosyne!" boomed the Duke as his bright cravat and even brighter head of red-gold hair swung past the two ladies. "How jolly to see you. I didn't even know you were here!" The pressure of matchmaking mammas and young ladies desperate to do something more than drink tea swept him onwards. He was gone before Mneme could do the polite thing and encourage him to talk to her friend.

"You know him personally," hissed Miss Agnew. "He called you by name!"

"He's my cousin," Mneme said heavily.

"Is that why you don't want to marry him? Because you know, quite a few lovely marriages do start out as family affairs…"

"It's more that I've met him," Mneme interrupted. She had already received several lectures this Season on why it was Perfectly Normal for cousins to marry. Mostly from her mamma, who would not let go of the image of Mnemosyne as the Duchess of Storm. "We wouldn't suit at all, is the thing. I'm sure he'll make someone an adequate husband, if their expectations are not unduly raised by the whole ducal title business, but that person shall not be me."

"Will you be my partner for croquet?" Miss Agnew asked after a long, thoughtful pause.

"As long as you understand that I shall be hitting my ball in the opposite direction of His Grace the Eligible Duke at all times."

"That's all right," said her new friend. "I can pine from afar."

THERE WERE ONLY two places where eligible young ladies in the polite society circles of the Teacup Isles could properly show off their magical abilities to marriageable gentlemen: the ballroom, and the croquet lawn.

The object of the game was to knock one's ball through the right hoops with a mallet. But six years ago, the very young Queen Aud was presented with a set of gold-plated croquet hoops as a coronation gift from the

distant Troilish Empire and almost caused a diplomatic
incident by declaring that croquet was the dullest pastime
in the world.

Alfred Lord Manticore, the Queen's Personal Advisor
on Magical Matters, saved the day by challenging the court
to a more "interesting" version of the game, after which
the traditional rules lurched rather dramatically into a
royal indulgence of chaos, charmwork and the gratuitous
application of hexes.

The unspoken rules of the new game made it a free-
for-all when it came to charms, enchantment, illusion or
any other forms of magic considered appropriate for
mixed company. One could not put a spell on another
player, or the lawn itself, but you could do so to any
mallets, hoops or balls that came within three feet of you.

The New Croquet was a splendid romp, when played
with imagination and gumption. It was also, as was true of
any pastime enjoyed at garden parties, house parties or
other gatherings of eligible unmarried gentlefolk, an excellent opportunity for creative flirting.

Mneme and Miss Agnew were both, as it turned out,
very quick with a mallet. They entertained themselves
knocking around a ball which flicked back and forth
between being a rolled-up hedgehog and a grass-covered
coconut macaroon.

Every other eligible lady in the garden party orbited
the Duke of Jupiter, as if he needed the attention. Their
spells were a riot of hearts, flowers, teasing word games
and attempts to be memorable while demonstrating no
originality whatsoever.

"You can join the crowd, you know," Mneme assured
her new friend. "I won't think any less of you."

"I'm hoping to gain points by being aloof and mysterious," Miss Agnew shot back, clipping the hedgehog gently

through another hoop, which hissed at her exactly as if it were a snake. "Oh, crumbs," she said, staring at it in alarm.

"Brace yourself," Mneme warned in an undertone as a certain mamma broke away from the gaggle of lace-shawled chaperones, chuffing towards them with a bosom that was incapable of doing anything other than heave.

"My dear," Mrs Galatea Seabourne gasped as she reached her daughter. "The best of news! The Duke has invited you and mousy little Metis to his house party next week. A house party, Mnemosyne! For a whole fort-night."

"What fun," said Miss Agnew with a hint of jealousy.

Mneme made a pained expression. "You promised me this was the last one, Mamma. You promised we could go *home*." Mneme adored the Seabourne family home. They had a modest library, a lovely garden, a very competent cook, and most important of all: no horde of people trotting through the house at all hours, demanding that she audition for the role of future wife.

Home was quiet and peaceful and calming in a way that the flurry of Society was not. If marriage could not offer her that, then she was in no hurry to be married; and to a Duke least of all.

"It's the end of garden party season, of course I promised this was the last one," said her mamma with a careless wave. "House party season begins. And you will be a guest of the Duke! Why, as his cousin I expect you will be top of the table if that interfering Lady Lovage doesn't take against you…"

Mneme groaned. This was clearly a battle she would never win. "If I agree to go to Cousin Henry's house party without complaint, I needn't attend any others, need I?" she tried.

"That all depends if you have a ring on your finger by

the end of it!" declared her mamma, who was nobody's fool. Mrs Seabourne turned around and trotted back to the game, neatly side-stepping two croquet hoops which had been charmed to dance a minuet together.

"You know what you have to do," said Miss Agnew in a low voice, as they both watched Mrs Seabourne cross the croquet lawn.

Mneme sighed heavily and nodded. "I have to find the Duke a suitable wife." She paused. "I don't suppose you were invited to this dreadful affair?"

Miss Agnew's eyes sparkled. "Perhaps if someone put in a good word for me...?"

CHAPTER 2

The only bright spot of this whole wretched house party business was that the Duke's main country residence Storm North was (as the name suggested) on the north side of the Isle of Storm, only a short boating journey from the Agnew estate on the Isle of Thyme.

Mneme found boating almost as tiresome as Town and Society — there was a wretched drawn-out jolting about the whole business, not to mention the harried running about with chests of clothes and sails and whatnot.

If only ladies were allowed the gentleman's prerogative of popping about from isle to isle by portal magic, instead of being squashed into pretty swan-shaped boats and lace-edged peacock carriages, the thought of marrying a Duke might not be so loathsome to Mneme.

But this was the world they lived in: one where ladies travelled by the slow path, while gentlemen were allowed short-cuts.

All the better to trap you with, my dear.

House parties were even more intense vehicles of the marriage market than garden parties. Having committed to a set period of time — a week, a fort-night, sometimes as much as a month — you were then shuttered up in a grand estate, chaperoned within an inch of your life, and placed beneath a magnifying glass of scrutiny by said chaperones while you engaged in the traditional mating dance of gentlemen and gentlemen's daughters.

Henry Jupiter, Duke of Storm, was clearly of a mind to be married, if he was bothering to host a house party of his own instead of hurling himself upon the hospitality of his chums. He was smart enough not to invite either of his living Aunts take on the vital role of hostess, which would have fallen to his own matchmaking mamma, the Dowager Duchess Antiope, were she still in the land of the living.

Still, this was Henry Jupiter, whose attention span was so short he often commissioned a new wardrobe in the middle of a Season because he was bored with the colours he had liked only a month earlier. It was by no means guaranteed that he would continue in the market for a wife if a suitable one did not win his eye instantly. After all, a Duke's life was one of wealth and freedom; without a mamma alive to harry him about the succession, he might put off matrimony for a decade or more.

Mnemosyne had an awful vision of the future, should she remain on the shelf: once she reached an appropriately hopeless age like twenty-eight, she would be in the ideal position to manage Henry's house parties and other personal events (no need to hire a hostess with a spinster cousin at your beck and call!). She would thus be expected to spend most of her time either in Town, guarding his social diary and batting young gold-diggers away with a stick, or lurching from one island to the next in boats and carriages, to keep up with his whims.

She might as well marry him if that were the case: one gilded cage was much the same as another.

Mneme had no objection to marriage: she simply wanted a husband more biddable and less cosmopolitan than the grandiose Henry Jupiter. A gentleman's son who liked books and did not insist she go boating more than one week a year was her personal ideal. Unfortunately, those sorts of gentlemen weren't allowed anywhere near her, thanks to the calculating ambition of Mrs Galatea Seabourne and her determination that her only daughter marry a Husband of Note.

Having a new friend in the house might make the whole situation less dire. A word in the ear of his Grace's hired hostess and godmother, Lady Lovage, had the desired effect: Miss Letty Agnew was added to the waitlist of the house party, which proved lucky when one of the invited guests — a foreign Countess whom many suspected of being a secret jewel thief — became ill on the road and never made it to Storm North.

If it was Mneme awaiting the possibility of a last-minute invitation, she might have suspected her mamma of engineering the Countess's complaint, but Lady Agnew was all innocence as she escorted Letty to the room beside Mneme's, shaking the travel salt from the hem of her cloak. Letty herself looked flustered and embarrassed but not totally mortified, which was the best one could hope for, given the circumstances.

Truly the greatest achievement of Mneme's life thus far had been convincing her own mamma that her presence as chaperone at house parties would do more harm than good to her marriage prospects. Instead, she hired Mrs Paula Daze to do the honours: a quiet soul who was a lady novelist in her spare time and, as one would hope in a professional chaperone, highly adept at getting one out of awkward social situations.

~

THE FIRST SUPPER of the house party was amiable enough:
the invited ladies and gentlemen circled each other with
polite coos, never forgetting that their role was to allow the
Duke to shine.

There were five eligible ladies in their party, and Henry
had picked four hearty (but not too threatening) fellows as
his official chums, as well as several gentlemen from the
village to make up the numbers with the chaperones at
mealtimes.

It was exactly like every other first supper of every
house party Mneme had ever attended, until she excused
herself to replace a slightly blancmange-stained glove, and
found a man searching her bedchamber.

They had not been introduced, though he was at the
supper table earlier, one of the extra gentlemen clearly not
intended to be of interest to the eligible ladies. A secretary,
she assumed, or a solicitor; someone in trade, welcomed
into Henry's home as a trusted employee or friend. He
dressed in dark grey, with a tightly-tucked cravat several
years behind the fashion.

Caught with his hand between the pallets on her bed,
the man paused for only a moment and then stood with
polite grace. He was not handsome; he had what Aunt
Hecate would call 'an intelligent face,' not as a
compliment.

It occurred to Mneme that in this situation, a polite
lady ought to scream, though the ramifications of such a
noise were bound to be irksome to them both.

The man held up both hands. "My apologies for the
intrusion. I am here on the Duke's business."

"Believe me," said Mneme before she could properly

think out her retort, "the Duke of Jupiter has no business in my bedsheets."

She felt the flush take over her face almost instantly; the curse of the Seabournes was that their red-gold hair always came with pallid complexions, prone to blushing and freckles at the slightest provocation. The latter could sometimes be bleached away with milk and magic; the former, not so much.

"So I guessed," said the man with a quirk of his mouth. "Miss Seabourne, are you aware that you are the only eligible lady in this household whose bedchamber was not rife with baubles, gee-gaws, poppets and curse-dollies, intended to charm the heart of our friend the Duke?"

"Oh, that's who you are," said Mneme in some relief. "You're the spellcracker. Mamma said his Grace had hired someone to deal with all that necessary business. She was most disappointed." Not that it made any difference; Mneme had long ago learned to check her suitcase three times for unwarranted magical interference before she went anywhere near her cousin the Duke, or any other high-ranked gentleman. It was in everyone's best interests.

Truly, a magically talented mamma was a terrible thing to endure.

"Mr Charles Thornbury," said the spellcracker, nodding his head in brisk greeting. "Am I to understand that you do not wish to employ any unfair means in winning the hand of the Duke? It's remarkably sporting of you, I must say."

"Not at all," said Mneme calmly. "If there was an easy magical means to ensure that I did *not* win the hand of Cousin Henry, you may rest assured that I would employ it without guilt."

She did not miss the expression that crossed Mr

TANSY RAYNER ROBERTS

Charles Thornbury's face for a moment, as if he was impressed. She refused to be warmed by such attention. Clearly, Thornbury spent most of his professional life being disappointed by the behaviour of refined ladies. A brief reprieve in his regard was nothing to write home about.

"In that case, Miss Seabourne," said the spellcracker, clicking his heels as he bowed. "I take my leave. There are a few more beds to be divested of magical items before my evening's work is over."

"Don't let me keep you," she replied, equally politely.

It was the first time she had ever conversed with a man privately, and when the door closed behind him Mneme had to admit to herself, just for a moment, that it was rather thrilling.

CHAPTER 3

Sympathetic magic was fair game in the courting dance and the marriage market; after all, the mesmeric effects of a curse-dolly or a carefully placed posy of herbs were known to be mild in effect. One could not make a person fall in love with you no matter how many times you kissed a woven piece of straw with their hair tangled in it, or whispered sweet nothings to a letter written in their personal hand.

Sympathetic magic could wield more intensity, if the magic-user was especially strong in the art, but those cases were rare. To previous generations such magical tricks were considered entirely appropriate to 'help things along,' the equivalent of pinching your cheeks to look rosy, or pouring the brandy with a heavier touch if one thought a proposal might be in the offing.

Perhaps Mr Charles Thornbury might consider the liberal use of brandy 'unfair means' of winning a husband also. Perhaps he might judge the pinching of cheeks. Mneme knew of a hundred chaperones and matchmaking

mammas who would disagree with him, but she rather
liked his sense of honour.

Of course, Thornbury was charged with protecting the
most eligible gentleman of the Teacup Isles from a veritable horde of thirsty young ladies: a marriageable Duke
under forty years of age who still had his own teeth did not
come along every Season. In his line of work, cynicism was
inevitable.

THE FIRST WEEK of the house party passed in a flurry of
organised entertainments, formal meals, and whispered
gossip. With the Countess a no-show, the front-runner in
the courtship of the Duke of Storm, was Lady Liesl of
Sandwich, fourth daughter of the sitting Earl of Sandwich,
and the Season's acknowledged Most Valued Player. She
was beautiful in a slender pale sort of way, quietly witty,
and seemed to think Henry was marvellous.

A surprise second horse in the race for his affections
was Mrs Juno Von Trask, a bold widow with a sultry voice,
an impressive bosom and a quick mind for card games.
She ran rings around Henry, challenging him at every turn,
and when he wasn't rendered speechless by the pallid
beauty of Lady Liesl, he was clearly one veiled innuendo
away from kissing the ungloved hand of Mrs Von Trask.

Mneme's 'mousy' Cousin Metis, who had finally
managed to leave Aunt Hecate at home in favour of a
hired chaperone for the first time since she came Out, was
something of an enigma. Mneme had always assumed that
Metis felt as she did about the possibility of marrying their
Cousin Henry: he was too loud, too sociable, too attached
to Town and its entertainments to make an appealing
husband.

But Mneme had underestimated how desperate Metis was to get out from under the thumb of Aunt Hecate and her machinations. As the week went on, Cousin Metis worked diligently to gain traction with the Duke. She did remarkably well thanks to some cleverly-placed witticisms, a few calculated moments of socially-appropriate intimacy, and a flattering new blue bonnet that made her eyes sparkle in the sunshine.

Mrs Von Trask and Lady Liesl were at their best during parlour games and at the supper table, but Cousin Metis had the edge with daytime activities, thanks to her physical skills at charmed croquet, archery and riding, not to mention her uncanny sense of timing which meant that, more often than not, she ended up partnered with Henry.

For the first time in years, Metis Seabourne had colour in her cheeks. It was fascinating for Mneme to watch, even if she knew she would never hear the end of it from her mamma if 'mousy' Cousin Metis snagged Henry's hand.

Miss Letty Agnew realised early on that the Duke of Jupiter had very little interest in her particular charms. Rather than invest too much in a horse race where she would inevitably come in fourth, she bowed out gracefully, and promptly caught the attention of two of Henry's invited friends: Colonel Winterbourne (moderately hand-some, and of moderate fortune), and Simon St Swithins, doctor of the village (delightfully shy, painfully poor, and clearly head over heels for young Letty).

There was quite a deal of entertainment to be had in watching Lady Agnew's contortions in trying to keep Dr St Swithins away from Letty, while hurling her in the path of the Duke and Colonel Winterbourne as often as possible.

Mneme could have told Lady Agnew that this was a sure way to end up with a village doctor as a son-in-law, but no one asked her, so she stayed quiet on the subject

except when agreeing with Letty that Dr St Swithins did
indeed have dreamy eyes (a verifiable fact).

∼

BY FAR THE strangest aspect of this long, busy week was the
accidental friendship Mneme somehow acquired with a
certain spellcaster.

Once she noticed the existence of Mr Thornbury, he
was *everywhere*. At the croquet pitch, in the day parlours and
the evening parlours. Most especially he was in the library.

The ladies retired to Storm North's magnificent library
after breakfast every morning, for their daily correspondence with relatives and friends. Without fail, Thornbury
would be there, busily researching something, pointedly
removing a curse from some item or other belonging to the
Duke, and ensuring that no lady of the house party went
anywhere near the section of the library reserved for texts
on love spells, compulsion spells or sympathetic magic.
(Based on what he had apparently confiscated over the last
few days, very few of them needed to consult books for
further study, in any case.)

If Thornbury wasn't in the library he was elsewhere in
the house, constantly vigilant for any cases of wrongdoing
around his employer… and he took a great pride in
informing Mneme of the latest developments and discov-
eries of his work.

She wasn't sure why, at first, but she could not deny
that she found it compelling. She had collected almost
enough anecdotes to write her own treatise on the use of
minor charms in foiled wooing attempts.

Before long, she began sharing her own information.
After all, she wanted Henry to be happy in his marriage,
and one must presume it was better he had some say in

who his future bride was to be, instead of leaving it in the hands of whomever was canny enough to outwit Mr Thornbury.

"His Grace's hairbrush went missing today," Thornbury confided in Mneme, as she passed his desk in search of a new novel.

"Lady Liesl's embroidery hoop has some suspicious red hairs caught up in the stitches," she told him in response, the following morning. "And I'm pretty sure Mrs Von Trask's letters to her sister just consist of the words 'The Duchess of Storm' written out over and over."

"I cleared three portraits of eligible ladies out from under His Grace's favourite chair this evening," he told her once after supper.

"The lavender bush in the East Shrubbery has been plucked bald," she informed him at the same time. "Keep a look out for charmed nose-gays and handkerchief bundles under his pillow."

"They want him to dream of them," Thornbury said with a smirk.

"Wasting their time," Mneme sighed. "I'm certain Henry dreams of nothing but horses and breakfast."

It was fascinating: the lengths to which the ladies were prepared to go to capture a Duke. Mneme had known such things happened, of course, but had never quite been this invested in the game.

"Don't do that," she said sharply to Metis one morning, when she caught her cousin early in the breakfast room, attempting to smuggle a lock of her own hair into the cushion of the seat at the head of the table. "That's the first place Thornbury will look. You're better off putting it in a random chair and coming up with an excuse for the Duke to sit there at the last moment."

"What would you know?" Metis sulked, but she did as Mneme suggested.

The Duke was delighted at the notion of swapping chairs at breakfast. Thornbury only caught on at the last second, whisking the cushion away from beneath the ducal arse and disposing of it with an expressionless face.

"I thought you weren't playing," he muttered later, catching Mneme's arm as she followed the others out for croquet. His fingertips were warm enough she could feel their heat through the butter muslin of her sleeve.

"You want it to be a challenge, don't you?" she teased, and almost tossed her head at him before realising that she should not flirt with a man she did not intend to marry.

"Bring it on," he said in a voice that sounded more charmed than annoyed.

Uh-oh.

CHAPTER 4

It would have carried on just like that, Mneme expected — foiled charms, an unwed Duke, and a shared interest with the spellcracker that edged a little too closely into inappropriate flirtation.

Everything changed when she received a note folded into a paper bird that slid under her door at midnight, flew up on to her canopy and fluttered at her until she awoke.

Come to the library as a matter of urgency.
Thornbury.

Mneme had a choice to make in that moment. What she should do, of course, was ignore the impertinent note, or at the very least wake her chaperone to ensure that a late night visit to the Duke's library did not compromise her utterly.

But Mrs Paula Daze had been up late working on her latest novel, and was likely to be sleeping soundly.

The thrill of the invitation was overwhelming. After a moment's consideration, Mneme decided she could risk being compromised, just a little. If it was ever going to happen to her, she wanted it to be in a library.

She wrapped herself in her best dressing gown, and the especially modest nightgown that her mamma demanded be let down so that it did not show her ankles.

If she was going to be compromised, Mneme wanted to make sure that her ankles, at least, were saved for her wedding night.

ALL THOUGHTS of an illicit encounter were swept away when Mneme arrived in the library to find the lanterns burning. Thornbury leaned over a map of the Teacup Isles, his shirtsleeves rolled indecently high and his hair uncombed.

A disgruntled maid stood refilling a teapot in the corner; no risk then of Mneme being compromised tonight. She was almost disappointed.

"Ah," said Thornbury, glancing up at her with his eyes wild. Goodness, his chin looked like it needed a shave. Was that common for menfolk in the dead of night? How had she ever thought he wasn't handsome? "There you are. I need your help. The Duke of Storm has been kidnapped."

The maid gave a small squeak, and rattled the teacups in the corner.

Thornbury's forehead creased charmingly, between his eyes. "I misspoke," he said quickly. "That is to say — he has eloped, and I am hoping to prevent it getting as far as the altar until I am certain it is a choice of his own free will."

"An elopement does rather sound like Henry," Mneme winced. "My cousin tends towards the impulsive, as you know."

22

"I know," said Thornbury, dragging his hands messily through his hair, an action that only served to make him look like a ruffian. "But I made him swear on his father's grave that he would not attempt an elopement this Season — that he would allow me to be *present* for any wedding, to ensure there was no magical interference."

"Oh, he hated his father," Mneme said absently. "You should have made him swear on something he cared about, like the graves of the four dogs called Ruffles."

Thornbury stared wildly at her as if she was not being remotely helpful. "You think he *hasn't* been kidnapped by one of the ladies?"

Mneme sighed. "No, you're right, kidnap is the likeliest solution. Have you been able to locate him?"

One of the easiest and most common types of sympathetic magic was locating a person on a map; the look on Thornbury's face made it clear that this was eluding him tonight. Failing as such a basic spell must hurt his pride something shocking. "A powerful force is shielding him from all magical attempts at location."

"That's unfortunate."

"Indeed." He gazed at her, his eyes bright with hope. "We have a narrow window of opportunity. No priests will perform services in the middle of the night, which means we have until dawn to seek, locate and retrieve the Duke of Storm. Can you help me?"

"Sympathetic magic has never really been my strength…" admitted Mneme, her eyes still fixed to the map.

"No," Thornbury coughed. "I mean, could you discreetly check the bedrooms and see which of the ladies is missing? Knowing whom he is with might give us a clue about where he has gone."

"Oh," said Mneme, blushing horribly. "Yes, I can do

23

that." Foolish to think she had anything to offer a spell-cracker of his calibre other than being a lady, who had access to the sleeping quarters of other ladies. "Can I take the maid with me?"

"Yes," he said, waving a hand and already staring back at his map, losing interest in her. "I fetched her for you."

LESS THAN HALF AN HOUR LATER, Mneme and the maid (her name was Sadie, she had five sisters, and one or other of them was always running off with some fellow, so midnight mercy dashes were nothing new to her) returned to the library.

Thornbury had not moved from his unhelpful map in all that time. If anything, his hair was more tousled and his shirt-sleeves rolled up even higher than before. Otherwise nothing had changed. "Well?" he asked. "Which of our eligible ladies has flown the coop with her prize?"

"None of them," said Mneme, clearing her throat in the hopes he would look up sometime soon. "Lady Liesl of Sandwich, Mrs Juno Von Trask, Miss Metis Seabourne and Miss Letty Agnew were all soundly in their own beds, until I woke them with the query."

"That's curious," said Thornbury, half muttering to himself. "I wonder if we should consider…"

Mneme cleared her throat again, and this time he looked up.

"Ah," said Thornbury, seeing for the first time that Mneme and Sadie had not returned to the library alone. They were accompanied by (wrapped in an assortment of interesting dressing gowns) Lady Liesl of Sandwich, Mrs Juno Von Trask, Miss Metis Seabourne and Miss Letty Agnew. "Perhaps you misunderstood the task I gave you,"

Thornbury said levelly. "I am certain that it included the word 'discreetly'."

"No one screamed the house awake," said Mrs Juno Von Trask with her usual brand of arch sarcasm. "How much more discretion could we *possibly* achieve at this hour?"

"I didn't invite them," Mneme said quickly. "They just sort of... came along."

"I'm surprised none of the chaperones are here along with us," remarked Lady Liesl. "Are they so uncurious about this evening's events?"

Everyone looked at Mneme.

"I didn't wake the chaperones," she said. "Mr Thornbury only asked —"

"Oh, you silly biscuit," Cousin Metis said scornfully. "We're not the only people living under this roof who might benefit from landing a ducal husband. Not all of our chaperones have living husbands. Next thing you'll be saying you didn't check that all the maids were in their beds."

"I didn't think," Mneme started, furious at herself. Of course she should have thought of that.

Thornbury, just as guilty as she was of thinking small, threw up his hands in despair. "I was rather hoping that if no marriage has taken place, we might avoid the appearance of the Duke being compromised," he said impatiently. "In order to prevent an unwanted marriage. The fewer people who know about this attempted elopement, the better!"

"Too late for that," said Mrs Juno Von Trask, whirlwind strategist that she was. "Many hands make light work, or so my old nanny used to say. Teamwork, ladies!"

They set off on another bout of waking up the household, with Mneme, Letty and Sadie in charge of the maids and other female staff, while Juno and Cousin Metis followed up on the chaperones.

As Mneme was swept out of the library as part of a sea of female efficiency, she saw the lovely, talented Lady Liesl join Mr Thornbury at his map.

"Perhaps I can help you locate the Duke," Lady Liesl said in that gentle, perfect voice of hers. "After all, I am quite skilled in the art of sympathetic magic."

"I'm well aware," said Thornbury with a rueful smile. "Having discovered and disposed of so many of your attempts to enchant my Duke's heart."

"Can't blame a lady for trying," said Lady Liesl with a quirk of her rosebud mouth.

And Thornbury... well, he gave the lovely lady a look that Mneme had always rather assumed was meant only for her. A look that said: *go on, then, impress me.*

Mneme felt rather deflated as she went on with her task.

AFTER IT WAS DISCOVERED that the chaperones and the maids were all present and correct, someone thought to note that several islands now allowed gentlemen to marry gentlemen, which called for (with rather more careful chaperonage) all of the male house guests to likewise be roused.

The library was more crowded than it had been at any other point during the entire house party.

Just as someone remarked aloud that it might be time to count the footmen, Mr Thornbury hurled a silk poppet of his Grace the Duke at the third map to fail him that evening. "He's still shielded from my sight," he raged. "The only possible way to do that is if he is at one of the private estates with wards designed to screen for the privacy of residents — but even then, I *should* have broken through. Either an enchantress of immense power has laid new wards around the Duke, or..." He frowned. "Such magic is easier to accomplish if it's a place that is deeply imbued with personal significance to him."

"There must be dozens of temples here on the Isle of Storm, many of them on private estates," spoke up Mneme. "And we already sent Sadie's brother the stable-hand to check the temple here in the local village," she added, glad for once to have thought of something ahead of time. "He said there was no sign the Duke took a horse out at all."

"He travelled by portal," Thornbury said grimly. "Two people left his private portal upstairs several hours ago, but I couldn't get any information read on where they went."

That caused a bit of thrilled gasping to go around the room, because if the Duke had indeed been mesmerised by a lady of quality... well, portal travel was simply not the done thing for ladies.

Perhaps they were right to theorise that the Duke's kidnapper was not a *lady* after all.

"There are seven official ducal properties," Cousin Metis spoke up. "All of them significant to Cousin Henry, but also... rather obvious destinations."

"I could check them all," Thornbury said, sounding more defeated by the moment. "But if his kidnapper is half the enchantress I think she is, there will be a warning hex built into His Grace's personal portal, so that they will be alerted the second I use it. I need to be sure I'm headed to the right place, if I fire up that portal." He looked around the room, meeting the eyes of each lady. "Do any of you have suggestions of a temple on a private estate that means something deeply significant to Henry Jupiter?"

There was a long pause as all of the ladies considered how little they knew about the Duke that many of them had hoped to ensnare in marriage.

"His parents were married here at the local temple in the village," volunteered Mneme. "Aunt Antiope insisted, though it's a Seabourne tradition to…"

"His naming ceremony was at the Palace," interrupted Cousin Metis, not to be outdone. "Wistworia, not Bumbleton."

"I think we can be reasonably certain he's not at the Palace," sighed Thornbury.

"Perhaps you should ask Lady Lovage," spoke up Dr Simon St Swithins, who had taken up a station very close to Miss Letty Agnew, presumably hoping to ensure that if she was swept away by the events of the evening, he would be her first port of call for her own elopement.

Everyone stared at the good doctor, all realising in the same instant that in their consideration of eligible ladies, chaperones, maids and gentlemen, no one had thought to rouse the Duke's own hired hostess and godmother.

"Uh," said Dr St Swithins, clearly not used to such attention. "That is. I believe she was friends with his mother? She might have some intelligence to share."

"Better that than bring Mamma or Aunt Galatea in to consult," said Cousin Metis beneath her breath.

Mneme agreed fervently if silently with that particular sentiment.

"Well, someone go and get her!" demanded Mrs Juno Von Trask.

And that was how, at ten minutes past one in the morning, they all discovered that Henry Jupiter, the Duke of Storm, had eloped with Lady Europa Lovage, his godmother.

As the library descended into a hubbub of scandalised

gasping, muttering and complaining about how deeply many of the attendees felt the personal insult of the Duke's choice of bride, Mneme saw Mr Thornbury roll up his maps and quietly exit.

Of course, she followed him.

CHAPTER 5

"You shouldn't be here," Mr Thornbury told Mneme as she stepped into her cousin's boudoir (was it a boudoir if owned by a gentleman?) and found herself, for the second time this week, alone with the spellcracker in a bedroom.

"If you're worried about my marriageability, don't be," she said with false levity. "Once this story gets out, I'll be invited to every dinner party from now until eternity."

Thornbury gave her a ruffled, annoyed sort of look. "I'm glad this is all so entertaining for you. Please return to the library and rejoin your party. I have a job to do."

"No," said Mneme, and took another step into the room. Her heart was beating faster. This was the most scandalous thing she had ever done.

Despite her cynicism about the marriage market and Society, she *did* want to marry. She wanted a quiet life with a good husband, in a home similar to the one where she currently lived (when she was allowed to be away from the social whirl) well away from the control of her dear mamma. She wanted to be respectable enough that she was still invited to the weddings and naming days of her family members and friends.

If she did this, she might lose that future. She might end up ruined, not merely on the shelf. But Mneme had entered Society dreading the possibility that she might end up married to someone not of her choice. She could not let that happen to Cousin Henry if she had the means to stop it, even if he had grown up into the worst sort of self-satisfied peacock.

"I know where Lady Lovage has taken him," she informed Mr Thornbury. "And I'm coming with you."

"You are not," he said immediately. "Ladies cannot travel by portal, unmarried ladies especially. Not even married ladies with their husband's permission could hold their head up in public after such a scandal."

"Well, I'll have to petition the Queen for her forgiveness if I get caught," Mneme said desperately. "You can't do this without me."

"Why?" Thornbury demanded.

"Knowing it's Lady Lovage — well, she doesn't have a family estate any more, she lives in Town. So the most likely option is the family temple on the Seabourne estate on the Isle of Memory."

Thornbury frowned. "Your father's estate."

She did not question how he knew that for certain; clearly he had rigorously checked the backgrounds of all the ladies invited to the house party... including the one whom the Duke had hired to run the affair. Lady Lovage was short on funds since her late husband's demise years ago, which was why she hired herself out as a hostess in the first place. Her country estate had been the first to be sold off.

"The fastest way to get there is using the portal in my father's private library," said Mneme. "You can't access it without an invitation. You certainly can't make it through the estate wards on the house and grounds without being accompanied by a member of the family." She caught her breath, waiting.

"Are you sure," Thornbury began to say.

"It all fits," she insisted, eager to share her working out. "You said she would only be able to hide him this well if he was to be married on a private estate, if the location was of significance to him. Henry *loved* playing in our family temple as a boy. We used to run away from our fussing mammas and play castles there. He never had a chance to play at home because everyone was always reminding him that he was going to be a Duke someday."

Mneme was overtaken by a wave of nostalgic fondness for her cousin, ridiculous man that he was now. Little Henry loved the temple on the Isle of Memory best of all, because of the wild ocean view and the fact that the temple was on high ground, just far enough away that he and Mneme and Metis could play out of sight of the grownups. She had forgotten about those games, about Henry's little face sulky and cross when his mamma dragged him about in that starchy suit, paying calls on her sisters.

He did not come alive until he was out of her sight, with his jacket off and his hair blowing in the sea breeze.

The Seabourne sisters, Galatea and Hecate and Antiope… ladies of such a proud magical lineage that when they all came Out in the same Season without a single dowry between them, two of them quickly caught gentlemen who were more than willing to change their name upon marriage; and the third, of course, married a Duke.

Lady Lovage was there sometimes too, Mneme recalled, gossiping over mint tea and tiny savouries, though her little girls were younger and duller than the Seabourne cousins, and simply terrible at playing castles…

Oh.

Mneme closed her eyes for a moment. "Lady Lovage has four daughters," she whispered. "Four daughters with no dowries." Of course. Now it made sense.

"Thank goodness for that," said another voice, breaking into their conversation. "So the old bat doesn't want to steal our Duke for *herself*?" It was Cousin Metis, highly amused at catching her cousin alone with the spellcaster. "I do hope I'm not interrupting something?"

"I'm trying to talk Miss Seabourne out of doing something that would greatly damage her reputation," said Mr Thornbury.

Cousin Metis smiled in a sly sort of way that she rarely shared in mixed company. "Mneme, are you trying to have all the fun? Back in a minute." She slipped away as quickly as she had arrived, leaving Mneme staring desperately at Mr Thornbury, and once again without a chaperone.

"Why are you doing this?" he asked in a low voice that made her spine tighten as if she were wearing old fashioned corsetry beneath the nightgown.

"Because," Mneme replied. "No one should marry the wrong person."

"This is Society," Mr Thornbury said, sounding weary. "Ladies and gentlemen marry the wrong person all the time."

"I won't," Mneme said with more confidence than she had ever felt on the matter. "And neither will Cousin Henry if I have any say in it."

Thornbury gave her a tight smile. "Your optimism is noted."

Mneme snatched up a piece of ducal stationery from the nearest chest of drawers and scribbled a few lines on it:

***The bearer of this letter is an invited guest to the
private estate of Shellwich Standing
on the Isle of Memory
by Miss Mnemosyne Seabourne and family.***

She signed it with a flourish, infusing the signature with her own magical pattern. It was a common form of sympathetic magic, the personal invitation. Like private letters and oaths in blood, it opened doors that otherwise might remain closed — in this case, it should give Mr Thornbury full portal access to her family home and the wider estate.

A lady might not be allowed to use portals without dire social consequences, but her correspondence skills were essential to the smooth running of the portal network.

Thornbury accepted the letter with gratitude and held it up to the portal, warming up the magic necessary to make his voyage. *Their* voyage, Mneme was determined, though he still had not agreed to take her with him.

The Duke's portal resembled a full-length mirror, with a slightly wider girth than was necessary for a standard reflection. Mneme had often wondered if the reason ladies were prohibited from the most convenient form of travel in the first place was because the wide skirts and gravity-defying wigs of the previous generation's fashions would have made it impossible to squeeze through a standard frame.

As a vortex of swirling purple and green lights began to form in the portal, Mneme heard a lady-like clearing of a throat, and looked up.

Cousin Metis was back, still in her nightgown, though she had thrown a shawl over the top of it as if this might fool anyone into thinking she was properly dressed. She was accompanied by Lady Liesl of Sandwich and Mrs

Juno Von Trask, who were just as improperly attired and looked equally pleased with themselves.

"Oh, no," said Thornbury, when he turned and saw them arrayed in the doorway. "I simply cannot allow…"

"It's amusing that you think you have a say in the matter," said Juno in a voice that made it clear she did not find it even slightly amusing.

"Consider us mutual chaperones," said Cousin Metis with an arch look at Mneme.

"Speak for yourself," said Lady Liesl in her lilting, lovely voice. "I still intend to capture myself a Duke."

"I could lose my license if the Queen discovers I allowed four ladies to use a portal, let alone a private gentleman's portal…" Thornbury protested.

"The Duke of Storm is one of the Queen's favourites, is he not?" said Metis. "I'm sure she'll be very grateful he was rescued. Speaking of gratitude, I don't want Cousin Mneme to be the only eligible lady involved in his Grace's rescue. He's likely to try to marry her on the spot the second he comes to his senses, all the more so if she has been compromised."

"Good point," said Mneme, who hadn't even thought of that ghastly possibility. "And thank you."

"It's entirely selfless on my part," said Metis, smiling with all her teeth.

"We intend to make sure the Duke has a choice of ladies to bestow his gratitude upon," said Juno. "It's only fair."

Thornbury shook his head and turned back to work on the portal again, the magic humming like a pianoforte as he tuned and readied it.

Mneme took the opportunity to catch her cousin's sleeve and draw her to a far corner of the room. "What are you really plotting?" she whispered. "You aren't still setting your cap at Cousin Henry?"

"Never mind me, I know what you're up to, Mnemosyne Seabourne," Cousin Metis whispered back. "You think that if you bruise your reputation just enough, you might be able to convince your papa — if not your mamma who would overdose on smelling salts rather than let it happen — to let you lower yourself to a *professional* husband. A spellcracker, perhaps?"

Mneme blushed hotly. "Don't be so vulgar. Professionals are no better or worse than gentlemen, and they are a far sight more useful to the world. Any lady would be lucky to have a capable, talented man like Mr Thornbury as a husband. But it won't be me."

Metis blinked, surprised at this turn of events. "Why on earth not?"

"Look at him," Mneme hissed with a hand-gesture that was far from discreet. Luckily, Thornbury was so caught up with his work, and distracted by an ongoing argument with Juno and Lady Liesl that he didn't notice a thing. "He's the Duke of Storm's man. His life will be a constant whirl of drama, disaster, politics and Society events, darting between Town and Court and the various ducal estates and commitments. Marrying him would be just as bad as marrying Henry himself. The future Mrs Thornbury, like the future Duchess of Storm, will either spend half her life in lace carriages and swan boats, or stuck at home with the children. Either way, she'll barely see her husband from one week to the next."

"I thought you were longing to be stuck at home," said Cousin Metis impatiently.

"I want more than that from a marriage," confessed Mneme, her eyes returning to the strong, capable figure of Thornbury in his shirtsleeves.

Cousin Metis scoffed at her. "We don't all get what we want. Do you think I want to marry Cousin Henry or some other lord like him?"

Mneme took her cousin's hand and gazed with fondness at her face, so like her own. Neither of them had a sister. Why weren't they closer? "You deserve more from life than merely escaping your mamma," Mneme said with love. "Expect more, Metis."

"There's something seriously wrong with you," sighed her cousin, but when Mneme hugged her on impulse, Metis hugged back.

Mr Thornbury had clearly lost the argument with Juno Von Trask. "The portal is ready," he announced with a general glower around the room. "But if Queen Aud or any other concerned citizen asks, I had *no idea* what the four of you were planning." He released the last unlocking charms on the portal, which sparkled with a constellation of colour. "I'm going to step through to Shellwich Standing, and the portal will be active for the ten minutes following my transportation. If any foolhardy ladies choose to follow me, it is none of my concern."

He practically threw himself through the portal, and was gone in an instant.

"Did Letty not wish to join us?" Mneme asked aloud.

"She decided against risking her reputation. Her mother was so grateful she stayed behind that Dr St Swithins started looking rather hopeful about his chances," said Juno. "Personally, I'm all for taking back the power. Let's make portal travel not only allowable for ladies, but fashionable. Shall we?"

Lady Liesl didn't hesitate, leaping into the portal like

she was entering a country dance. Metis followed, with Juno not far behind.

No going back now. Mneme hoped that Cousin Henry appreciated what she was risking on his behalf — and that he didn't appreciate it so much that he started getting funny ideas.

She took a deep breath, and stepped into the portal.

CHAPTER 6

*M*neme had never stepped through a portal before.

She recalled the first time she saw her father use his own, ducking out of the house for an appointment in Town, or for one of his many trips to 'take the waters' on the Isle of Bath. She recalled a strong breeze whipping up around the room, and a sense of dizzy pressure in her stomach as she got too close.

She had expected that when she stepped through she would experience a wash of cold energy, similar to the feel of ocean on bare feet or the chilly sensation of walking through high security wards.

Instead, portal magic came with a deep, pulsing heat that rippled across her skin, tightening all her nerves and then releasing in a wave of discomfort that verged on pleasure.

Mneme felt strangely empty as she landed safely on the carpet in her father's library.

"Well," said Juno, adjusting her hair and discreetly

39

fanning herself with her hand. "I have a new theory as to why they don't allow ladies this *particular* freedom."

It was an hour before dawn, the earliest possible time that a priest or priestess might be convinced to perform a wedding ceremony — and knowing the general crankiness of the clergy on the Isle of Memory, Mneme would be surprised if any marriage, even one involving clandestine arrangements or a special license, was achieved before nine.

At ten minutes past five on a Thursday morning, Mneme expected her family home to be entirely quiet. With her father away (Mr Seabourne generally used his wife's preoccupation with the Season as an excuse to disappear to the Isle of Bath) only her mother was in residence. Mrs Galatea Seabourne was a late sleeper and late breakfaster, so even the lowest-ranked maids would not be expected to climb out of bed for another hour or so.

It was therefore greatly surprising when Mneme and her guests stepped out of the library and into a veritable hive of activity. Every servant in the house, and many who were only hired from the village for special occasions, was already hard at work. Every light blazed. Orange blossom and myrtle fronds hung from each sconce and lintel.

"I take it the elopement is no longer a secret," said Juno when she saw the blatant nuptial flavour of the display.

"It's not an elopement," muttered Mr Thornbury, striding ahead to push open the doors of the grand dining room, the one that the family only dusted off for holiday parties. "It's a damned wedding."

Mneme gasped to see the tables decorated and laden with what could only be described as a splendid wedding breakfast: fresh rolls and fruit, sugared almonds, and jewel-coloured jellies matched with bright pastel junkets. There was a glazed ham set out on her great-grandmamma's best silver platter, and a whole tongue so large that it was presented across two china plates.

There was a table laden with metal dishes full of hot savouries, eggs and salmon, charmed to stay piping hot until they were needed. Another table set out only with teacups, ready to be poured.

And the cake — in the centre of it all, the wedding cake, like an extravagant bouquet of roses sneering down at the daisy bed below them.

Magic was everywhere. Mneme's house did not smell familiar to her at all, with so much power emanating from the decorations, the tables, and most of all, that cake. It had so many tiers it could be hollowed out and used as a human-sized portal. Each layer was thick with white almond icing, silver flowers and sugared beads. That cake was clearly the hub of the power that had taken over her house.

"It's more than one spell — many layered over each other," said Mr Thornbury. "Last time I witnessed a house this thick with power, it was necromancy, not sympathetic magic."

"Isn't sympathetic magic used for small things?" asked Lady Liesl. "Like charms or hexes. Nothing grand, nothing operatic…"

"That is usually the case," he agreed, looking distinctly worried.

"Lady Lovage must have hired a spellcaster, or an army of spellcasters," Juno said briskly. "I refuse to believe that woman is capable of a project of this magnitude on her own. Her croquet charms were never all that impressive."

"Or someone hired *her*," Cousin Metis said in a low voice. "To get the Duke here in the first place."

"Those are both viable possibilities," said Mr Thornbury, stepping closer to examine the cake. His breath caught in his throat.

Two figures stood atop the cake, sculpted in fondant. If you could use sympathetic magic to control a man's actions through a wax dolly or silk poppet, why not use one made out of sugar?

The bridegroom was clearly Cousin Henry, wearing his favourite plum top hat. Every whisker of his red-gold beard was carefully carved in place. With such attention to detail, it was no wonder that the spell held such resonance beyond the cake itself.

The bride was... and oh, Mneme saw now why Thornbury had reacted as he did. It was clearly not Lady Lovage, nor any of her unmarried daughters (unfashionably blonde, every one of them). When you got close enough to see the detail beneath the crown of sugar violets... this bride had red hair.

Mneme exchanged a startled look with Cousin Metis, who displayed equal surprise. She turned to meet Mr Thornbury's gaze, and saw an expression of utter fury cross his face, before it was replaced by a chilly kind of politeness that was even worse.

"You don't think —" Mneme began to say.

"I think that if I am to rescue our eloped Duke before he is wed without his consent, I should do it as I always intended," said Mr Thornbury with a polite bow. "*Alone.*"

Mneme could not blame him in the least for suspecting her, given the evidence. Henry Jupiter was about to be married from this house, to a bride with all the markings of a Seabourne. (But oh, it still hurt to see that moment of distrust in his eyes.)

"This is awkward," Juno Von Trask remarked, never one to let a silent moment go unchallenged.

Mneme opened her mouth for a moment to deny that she or her cousin were the intended bride, but she could not in all conscience make such a claim without being sure, absolutely certain, that neither her mamma nor Aunt Hecate was behind this plot. Both women were ruthless when it came to the pursuit of a good marriage for their daughters (even if they both fell down on efficacy) — and powerful magic did run in the family after all.

Mr Thornbury turned his attention back to the cake. He picked up a silver salt-shaker and threw a pinch of salt across the table, where the grains were incinerated in a flash by a protection spell so vicious, it would be considered overkill on the Queen's jewels. "Hmm," he muttered, as if this was exactly what he had expected.

"Mnemosyne!" carolled a voice from within the house — the unmistakably shrill tones of Mrs Galatea Seabourne, Mneme's mamma. "Jane told me you were here." The lady of the house burst through the doors, garbed in a frightful gown so covered in embroidery, ruffles and tassels that it practically screamed Mother Of The Bride. "There you are!"

"Here I am," said Mneme, bracing herself. There really was no proper etiquette for questioning one's mother about her involvement in a dastardly kidnapping and forced elopement.

"What are you wearing?" bellowed Galatea Seabourne, which was the pot calling the kettle full of boiling water. She seized Mneme's arm and steered her out of the dining room. "Best dress for weddings, my dear, don't you listen to a thing I tell you? Don't worry about your guests, I'll make sure someone takes care of them... You too, my dear," Mamma added suddenly, grabbing Cousin Metis in her other hand on their way out of the room.

Metis was clearly stunned at being spoken to nicely by an aunt who had always treated her like pond scum. Like Mneme, she allowed herself to be steered without protest.

Something was terribly wrong, Mneme finally acknowledged to herself as they were escorted upstairs in search of best dresses, despite knowing that all their good things were hanging in wardrobes back at Storm North. Mamma calling Cousin Metis 'my dear' was the most suspicious behaviour she had witnessed in years.

Had her mother orchestrated this whole mess of an elopement to secure Henry as a husband for Mneme? And if so, was it possible to climb out a third floor window?

Mneme had no chance to investigate her suspicions right this moment, because her mother had already led Mneme directly to her bedchamber and disappeared on whatever nefarious deeds she was up to. It all happened so quickly, like when a string quartet launches into a familiar dance at double the speed. Metis was nowhere in sight.

And...

There was a dress.

Not just any dress.

A *best* dress.

It was a high-waisted teagown in the classical silhouette, with three layers of soft, flowing fabric. Perfectly in fashion and expertly crafted, except that the colour (a rich red) was more suited for a merry widow or young, recently-married lady than a maiden who had not yet given up on the marriage market.

This might be her wedding dress. It was the most beautiful garment that Mneme had ever owned. If she ended up murdering her mamma, it wouldn't even show the stains.

~

"Don't you look lovely!" exclaimed Mrs Galatea Seabourne as Mneme emerged from her room, wearing the beautiful new dress. "Such a flattering colour!"

Mneme had a childhood memory full of reminders that her mamma hated to see her in any colour bolder than blush or cream.

Even now, she waited for the sting that inevitably followed the compliment. "You look so pretty BUT" or "your complexion is so flattered when you stand out of direct sunlight," or "if only your hair behaved itself you might get away with that style."

"Lovely," Mneme repeated when she realised that there was to be no follow up remark. She stepped closer to her mamma, examining her guileless face.

"Lovely," her mamma repeated, and smiled as if there was nothing in the world she had ever meant more. "Perfect," she added, which was a blow too far.

Mneme leaned in, looking for some sign of magical influence, or demonic possession. She knew to look for a jewel-like gleam in the irises, but what she saw instead was a floating, clouded sheen on the surface of her mamma's eyes.

The good news was that her mamma was not the villain behind all this. The bad news... Mrs Galatea Seabourne was clearly in the thrall of someone more powerful than she.

"Mamma," Mneme said sharply, hoping that her voice would break through the cloud. "What's happening?"

For a moment, her mamma crumpled. "Oh, Mnemosyne," she whispered. "I think your Aunt Hecate has done something dreadful."

Metis, Mneme thought worriedly. *Does that mean that Cousin Metis is the intended red-haired bride in this pantomime?* "What do you mean?" she entreated.

45

Her mamma shook her head and smiled far too brightly. "Come along, darling, mustn't be late. We have a wedding to attend!"

CHAPTER 7

$\mathcal{C}$ousin Metis waited for them in the hall below, also in a brand-new best dress, though this one was a deep sapphire blue. "Are you the bride?" Metis asked immediately, looking Mneme up and down with great suspicion.

"I was going to ask you the same thing," Mneme said sharply. Could Metis be in on this? Did she know her at all?

"Don't be silly," giggled Mamma. "You're both maids of honour for the new Duchess-to-be, of course."

The cousins turned, and stared at her.

"Mamma," said Mneme. "Who *exactly* is marrying Cousin Henry today?"

"Come along, hurry up!" Her mother seized each of them by an arm, and led them through the now-empty grand dining room, where no sign remained of the fancy wedding breakfast, or even the tables upon which it had been set out.

Mamma led them through the glass doors to the

garden, and along the winding path that led towards the small family temple.

Did the new best dresses have time-defying properties? It felt like hours must have passed since Mneme went upstairs to change. The servants had been busy, quite clearly, as the tables containing the entire wedding break-fast were now set out on the croquet lawn, along with a hundred or so white linen chairs, flapping in the breeze.

"Is Cousin Henry being married off by *elves*?" Mneme asked as they were rushed on past an acre of teacups, each brimming with tea and piping hot under a layer of preser-vation spells.

"Many hands make light work!" carolled Mrs Galatea Seabourne with the confidence of a middle-aged lady who had never worked a day in her life unless you counted fret-ting, catastrophising and matchmaking.

The wedding cake, still wrapped in all of its protection charms, towered over the tables of food and drink. It looked malevolent, vibrating with power barely contained by the layers of white sugar and almond paste.

Was it bigger than before? So many layers and so wide, it would never fit through a standard portal. Why, you could fit a person inside it…

Mneme dug her heels in, refusing to follow her mamma further until she had got a good look at that cake. A new fondant figure was stuck to the side of the cake: a man in dark grey, his face and limbs half-covered in thick marzipan.

"Mamma," Mneme said. "Where exactly is Mr Thornbury?"

"That man," said Mrs Galatea Seabourne. "I'm sure I don't know where he's got to."

The cake twitched.

Mneme let out a small gasp as if she had been slapped

and her mother — or whomever truly had control of her mother — swept her on again, along the garden path until they reached the incline that led up, up to the hill that had the best view on the island.

Here, for a second time, Mneme dug her heels in hard. "No, Mamma. I will not take another step until you tell me the name of Cousin Henry's bride-to-be."

"Me neither," chimed in Cousin Metis. "Good luck budging both of us, Aunt Galatea."

The spell clouding Mamma's eyes seemed to tighten its grip on her. She straightened her back, genuinely prepared to carry both young ladies up the hill to the temple if necessary. "My sister always wanted to be a Duchess," she declared dreamily.

"If you mean Auntie Antiope, she won that prize a generation ago when she married the Old Duke of Storm," Mneme said impatiently.

Cousin Metis had come to a very different conclusion. She was pale with shock, her freckles standing out furiously against her milky skin. "No," she breathed. "It's impossible. I wouldn't believe… *she's his aunt*."

Metis was up the hill in an instant, her deep blue dress caught by all the breezes as she hurried up the little marble steps inlaid in the slope, with all the athletic power of a young lady who learned fourteen different kinds of cotillion before she was Out.

"Metis, wait!" called Mneme, taking off after her cousin, leaving her mamma behind.

Cousin Henry and Aunt Hecate? Some aristocratic families residing in the Teacup Isles further away from Town and Court were infamous for intermarrying a little too closely from time to time, but *aunts* were always supposed to be off limits.

At the top of the steps, Mneme was dazzled by the

early morning sunshine hitting the bright white temple, with the backdrop of the prettiest piece of ocean this side of the Lyric Sea. They had been so happy here as children: Little Mneme and Little Henry and Little Metis, careless and relaxed and easily sunburnt with their matching pale skin.

Their mothers had gossiped on the lawn below, drinking tea while the children strayed higher and higher up those steps until they were blissfully out of sight.

Antiope, Hecate and Galatea Seabourne, famously three of the most talented magical women of their generation. All three came Out and were married in the same Season… and there was only one eligible Duke that year. Antiope caught him for herself, becoming the Duchess of Storm, and the other two found themselves genial, easy-going husbands who understood that becoming a Seabourne had a status to it only surpassed by the highest ranks of the gentry: the Earls and the Dukes.

Mneme had never seen this many people in her family's temple. There were hats as far as the eye could see. Guests sat on every stone bench, some of them squished up to make room.

The local priestess of marriages, estate planning and contract law stood in formal robes at the altar of Uranos and Gaia. Mneme wondered whether it had taken a hefty donation to the parish to get her here, or if her eyes were clouded.

Juno and Lady Liesl were in attendance, still in their nightrails as Mamma had apparently not seen fit to provide them with brand new gowns. It was hard to tell if they were enchanted or not.

She recognised many of the guests, even from the backs of their heads. Villagers, of course, and local dignitaries. A few of them looked around, seeming confused, but others sat rigidly on the benches, staring straight ahead. Mneme had never seen so much correct posture in her life.

Impossibly, the rest of Henry's house party were also in attendance. How had that happened? The gentlemen, Mneme might understand, but that was clearly Letty Agnew sitting between Lady Agnew and Dr Simon St Swithins. Had the Agnew mother and daughter cast away all propriety since four o'clock this morning, deciding it was no matter to travel by portal after all?

Metis still hovered on that top step, unsure what to do. Mneme squeezed her hand in what she hoped was a comforting manner. "We won't let this happen," she promised.

She could see Henry now. He stood, ramrod straight, at the altar with the priestess, and Mneme had no doubt that the cloud had been cast over him.

Everything about him that made him Henry — his pink cheeks and over-jovial manner, his silly jokes and loud booming laugh and expansive hand gestures — none of that was in attendance. Even his cravat was a dull shade of cream that entirely failed to clash with his red-gold beard. Mneme had never felt so attached to her cousin's usual pompous antics in all her life, now that she saw him stripped of his personality.

She was going to save him.

Lady Lovage and her daughters flocked around Henry, their matching blonde up-dos circled in orange blossom and myrtle. They looked as silly as ever, the whole gaggle, and Mneme was convinced that there was no cloud in any of their eyes. They were enabling this monstrosity of a wedding of their own accord, and every one of them looked horribly smug about it.

What did they expect to get out of this? Fresh-cut

dowries and endless favours from the incoming Duchess of Storm, perhaps?

Mr Thornbury was nowhere in sight and this, of all things, concerned Mneme the most. She could not forget that the cake had *twitched*.

"Where is she?" Metis asked beneath her breath, wringing her hands.

Music began: a small cluster of harpists and flautists concealed in a nearby shrubbery, producing a perfect lilting melody.

"I think we have to walk the aisle," said Mneme apologetically.

"I am not endorsing this farce," Metis snapped back, not bothering to keep her voice down. It bounced around the temple walls, echoing loudly. Hardly anyone winced.

Metis began the long walk down the aisle, marching like a soldier going to war. Someone placed a bouquet in her hands and she swung it back and forth like she knew, at some point, she would have to use it as a weapon.

Mneme scurried after her cousin, accepting a matching bouquet without complaint, wanting to get this part over with as quickly as possible.

It was easy to tell which guests were clouded and which were not by the small titters of laughter in response to Metis' behaviour. About half and half, then. Good to know.

Finally, the cousins reached the altar, exchanging uneasy looks.

The music swelled louder. Aunt Hecate came over the rise of the hill, every inch the triumphant bride. Mneme barely recognised her at first. With all the magic pinging back and forth around the grounds today, it should hardly be a surprise that Aunt Hecate had found the time to apply a Fountain of Youth charm to herself. (It might be months or even years before anything surprised Mneme ever again.)

Aunt Hecate had clearly overcooked the Fountain of Youth charm: she now appeared embarrassingly young, with rosy cheeks, pouting lips and long braids entwined with blossom. She barely looked old enough to be Out in Society.

Mamma came over the rise behind her, throwing handfuls of rose petals over her — now much younger — sister, with every appearance of wanting to be here. It occurred to Mneme that this entire situation would be doubly, triply mortifying if she did not know about the cloud in her mamma's eyes.

Aunt Hecate reached the altar, pushed back her floral braids, and simpered. Henry Jupiter, the Duke of Storm, looked utterly besotted with his bride. Mneme knew none of this was his fault, but part of her still squirmed with frustration at him.

"I have objections!" Cousin Metis announced loudly, as Henry and Aunt Hecate took each other's hands.

The priestess — clouded after all — ignored her, and began the formal chanting ritual, calling on the elements and the gods to bless their union. Cousin Henry didn't even flinch. The bride gave her daughter a sweet smile and bowed her head to the altar.

Cousin Metis turned to Mneme in a panic. "I don't know how to stop it. What do I do?"

Mneme had no idea. It all seemed so jolly when she and Mr Thornbury were catching out Henry's suitors with their tiny pieces of sympathetic magic, those subtle courting charms that nudged things along a bit, but were easily found and broken. She did not know how to begin to unwind a piece of enchantment this complex and powerful; and where was Mr Thornbury? Not here, that was for certain.

(The cake had twitched.)

"I don't know," Mneme admitted out loud. Something hit her foot. It was a croquet ball. A small, round, bright red leather croquet ball. She looked up, searching for its source and saw Letty Agnew, clearly unclouded, smiling impishly at her from the third row back.

"When in doubt, chaos," Mneme murmured, transforming the ball into a small, prickly hedgehog.

"What use is that?" Metis demanded.

"We're only limited by our imaginations," said Mneme, and threw the hedgehog directly into the face of the chanting priestess.

CHAPTER 8

It is true that a single hedgehog can do little in the face of awful and overwhelming power, but a hedgehog thrown in the right moment can be a call to arms — a declaration of chaos, like a cream bun hurled across a cafeteria, or a bridal bouquet tossed into a mob of hungry maidens.

As the hedgehog hit its intended target, Mneme turned and threw her bouquet to the benches. Dozens of ladies, trained in this manoeuvre their entire life, scrambled for the bouquet, leaving chaos in their wake.

Cousin Metis, getting the hang of this new plan very quickly, transformed her own bouquet into a generous cream cake and slammed it into the face of her youthened mamma.

Several more sticky desserts were hurled at the wedding party soon after, many of them coming from the direction of Letty Agnew, who looked utterly delighted with herself. Juno Von Trask stood on her chair and cheered, while Lady Liesl stole shoes from the guests sitting slack-jawed

near her, and transformed every shoe into a clucking,
feather-strewing hen.

Together, Mneme and Metis lunged for Aunt Hecate,
patting down her clothes and person in search of the
collection of poppets or other talismans she surely must
have about her person, to be clouding so many.

"Nothing!" huffed Metis, who had her mamma pinned
to the floor. As it turned out, a youthened Aunt Hecate did
not have the mighty grip or age-hardened ruthlessness of
her usual matronly self.

"We're looking in the wrong place," said Mneme. "I
think... no, I know where to look. Delay the wedding as
long as you can. That goes for all of you!" she hollered in a
most satisfying burst of noise as she scrambled to her feet.

As the riot of wedding sabotage expanded in a glorious
haze of croquet-style charmwork, Mneme picked up her
skirts and ran for it. Time to do what she should have done
when she first saw the wedding breakfast arrayed on the
lawn.

Time to rescue a spellcracker.

Of course it was the cake. With so many protection spells
woven around its giant, delicious sugared layers, it made
sense that the core of Aunt Hecate's spell was contained
within. The fondant dolls of the bride and groom were a
classic example of poppet magic, but Mneme wasn't
thinking of them right this minute. She was thinking of the
other fondant figure, the one stuck on the side of the cake.

Something she had learned from Mr Thornbury at the
house party: most magic is performed with no subtlety
whatsoever, and the method for undoing any given form of
unsubtle magic is usually rather obvious.

In this case: a cake.

Mneme headed straight for the teacup table. The only charms on that were to keep forty cups of tea at the perfect sipping temperature so that they might be distributed quickly as soon as the guests marched back down the hill from the temple. Such preservation charms were easily brushed aside.

(Mneme once had a governess who insisted it was essential that any lady know how to keep a cup of tea hot under any and all circumstances, so preserving spells were solidly inside her personal repertoire.)

She picked up a brimming cup in each hand, and threw them squarely at the wedding cake, one after the other.

It is a truth universally acknowledged that a cup of tea, forcibly applied to a powerful piece of magic, will have little to no effect. It is, however, a rare spell that is powerful enough to withstand several dozen full teacups of hot tea, thrown with gumption.

Mneme hurled cup after cup until her arm grew sore. The spell on the wedding cake hissed and fizzled with every blow after the tenth or so. After the twentieth, it began to shoot out sparks at one weak spot, near the base.

She aimed the cups firmly at that weak spot, continuing to throw until finally, at the thirty-third cup, the protection spell made a nasty whining sound, and dissolved into the air with the pungent odour of cinnamon.

Mneme ran up to the cake, caught in a brief moment of indecision as to whether she would free Henry or Mr Thornbury first. Trusting in Cousin Metis, Letty Agnew and the rest to keep Henry unmarried for as long as possible, she applied herself to the captured spellcracker.

Mr Thornbury, Mneme knew, had a special kit to deal with the unwinding and unravelling of poppets, wax dollies, hexbags and other pieces of sympathetic magic, to effectively break the connection that they made with the person affected by the spell.

She, on the other hand, was equipped only with her own two hands, a sense of righteous indignation, and one of the last remaining cups of tea, still closer to piping hot than tepid.

Carefully, she peeled the fondant poppet from the cake in which he was half-buried, untying strands of liquorice and sugar-root tangled around his middle. She dropped all of his bindings into the cup of tea, and then tapped the poppet on his head.

"Be free," she told him. "And I am truly sorry for everything my family has done to you."

The wedding cake coughed.

(How powerful a sorceress was her Aunt Hecate? Mneme had heard all the stories about what the Seabourne sisters were capable of in their youth, but she had still underestimated her, all these years.)

The wedding cake shuddered and broke apart from within, chunks of brandied fruitcake bursting forth through the layers of sugar and marzipan. Within the cake, a man.

Mr Thornbury was filthy as he emerged from his wedding cake cocoon. Mneme, who had never held a particular fondness for fruitcake, had the sudden wilful urge to kiss him, to see if she could taste all seventeen spices of their cook's famous recipe.

"Am I too late?" he asked in a rasping voice, taking leave of his gentlemanly manners long enough to spit a hunk of raisins on the lawn. Mneme emptied out the tainted cup of tea she was holding and fetched another, presenting it to him.

Thornbury drank the tea in one long gulp, which had

her paying more attention to his bare throat than was entirely proper. She had never seen a man so undressed before, much less one whose cravat had clearly been eaten by a wedding cake.

"Hopefully just in time," she answered, picking up the fallen fondant figure of Henry, and handing it to his spell-cracker.

Thornbury worked quickly, not bothering to waste time searching for his spellcracking kit. He located a single hair from Henry's natural head, where it was pressed inside the fondant of the poppet, and spoke quiet words of breaking and ending.

"Done," he said finally, and snapped the figure neatly in half.

A loud bellow resounded from over the hill, caught up in the echo chamber of the temple. Clearly Henry's sensibilities had now returned to him, as had the realisation that he was on the verge of marrying his aunt.

"She's clouded dozens of people," Mneme burst out. "Some of the servants, the local priestess, my mother… Were those enchantments in the cake too?"

"I don't think so," said Thornbury, taking stock of their surroundings. "Clouded, you say? Try the junkets."

They made for the table of moulded jellies and junkets, shimmering nearby. Thornbury did not hesitate to poke his long fingers inside the desserts, fishing out all manner of primitive poppets carved from apple or arrowroot biscuit. Methodically, with a great deal of instructive commentary from Thornbury, Mneme assisted him in releasing everyone on the estate from Hecate's clouding spell.

"I should apologise," said Thornbury quietly. "For doubting you, even for a moment, when I saw the hair colour of the bride poppet. I should have known better."

"That's the Seabourne redheads for you," said Mneme,

her light tone in direct contrast to the warmth that blossomed inside her chest. "Suspiciously pretty and smart... the women, anyway. The men are just pretty."

"I am lucky," said Thornbury, quite seriously. "That you placed your trust in me to unravel this mess. I wouldn't have blamed you if you left me stuck in that cake to teach me a lesson."

"Oh, I think you would have blamed me a little," Mneme said with great cheer.

They gazed at each other. Despite the fact that Mr Thornbury's skin, hair and clothes were still thoroughly marinated in crumbed fruitcake and brandy, Mneme thought that this would be an excellent moment to be kissed.

Naturally, that was when a furious Henry Jupiter came over the hill, flanked by his confused muddle of wedding guests, all clamouring for some kind of explanation. The moment was lost.

$\mathcal{H}$enry Jupiter, Duke of Storm, married Mrs Juno Von Trask six weeks later in a private ceremony, by special licence. No one was even a little surprised. After all he had been through, it made sense that he made his choice based on the bride's robust sense of humour.

The bride was thoroughly vetted by the Duke of Storm's private spellcracker, who declared that the future Duchess of Storm had exerted minimal magical influence upon her intended.

Everyone agreed that this was the best that could be hoped for, under the circumstances.

Neither of the Duke's living aunts were in attendance at the wedding, though his cousins Miss Mnemosyne and Miss Metis Seabourne were there, throwing rice on behalf of the family.

(It was rumoured that one of the Duke's aunts was in the Queen's custody awaiting kidnapping charges, but no one entirely believed such a shocking piece of gossip.)

The new Duke and Duchess of Storm hosted a

wedding breakfast one week later, in the grounds of Storm North, including a rather splendidly anarchic game of croquet which was won by the new Mrs Dr St Swithins (formerly Letty Agnew), narrowly beating Lady Liesl of Sandwich, who was getting rather used to coming in second.

Mnemosyne and Metis, close intimates of the new Duchess, shared a cup of tea with her on the lawn as the party continued around them.

"I'm a little disappointed there wasn't more of a scandal," drawled Juno. "In all the merriment, havoc and food fights, somehow the question about who travelled where by portal got entirely lost."

"Funny that," said Metis. "Not all of us have a ducal title to automatically get us out of hot water with the Queen," she added, without a hint of defensiveness.

Juno laughed that throaty laugh of hers. "Don't be sour, my dear cousin-in-law. I'm excellent at getting husbands, as it turns out. I'm more than willing to catch you one next."

"No rush," said Metis, whose eye had strayed to the pretty smile of Lady Liesl more often this afternoon than to any of the eligible gentlemen. "With my mamma busy on her... private business with the Queen, most of my reasons for marriage have become less urgent."

"Then how am I to reward you both for your heroic feat in rescuing my husband from a fate worse than death?"

Mneme smiled to herself, liking the way that Juno's arch tones softened whenever she said the words 'my husband.' It was turning out to be a good match. Even now, Henry turned from where he was chatting with the fellows across the lawn, and glowed as he exchanged a smile with his proud, sarcastic wife.

"I have an idea," Mneme said. "And I hope you're exceedingly grateful about the service we performed, because it's no small request."

"Do tell," said Juno, her eyes narrowing.

"I think it's time that ladies of nobility campaigned for the right to portal travel," said Mneme.

Juno laughed, long and loud. "Well," she said, when she had recovered. "I did say I wanted a scandal."

NO CAKE or junkets were served at the wedding breakfast of the Duke of Storm and his new Duchess. The happy couple requested savouries only, starting a trend that would resonate through the Teacup Isles for years to follow.

Thus, it was over sardines on toast and a cup of tea that Miss Mnemosyne Seabourne renewed her acquaintance with Mr Charles Thornbury, the Duke's spellcracker.

Politely, he asked after the health of her mother and father, who were not in attendance.

"They are both well," she assured him. "My mother has taken to the healing waters of the Isle of Bath, to the great disappointment of my father, who has long considered it his private sanctuary. He has taken up mountain hiking in retaliation. In any case, they are both far from home, leaving the family library as my personal domain."

He smiled warmly, which quite erased the usual creases on his work-worn brow. "That sounds exceedingly pleasant."

"It is exactly how I wished to spend the rest of the summer," Mneme assured him. "After so much excitement, I would be quite happy if I never had to ride in a swan-shaped boat or lace-edged peacock carriage ever again."

"Indeed," said Mr Thornbury, passing her a plate of

cress sandwiches and devilled eggs. "Is the library of Shell-wich Standing to be the headquarters of your portal equality campaign, then?"

"Oh," said Mneme, feeling the warmth as her cheeks coloured. "You heard about that."

"I did," he replied. "The Duchess of Storm has requested I make myself available to the committee, given that my duties of protecting the Duke from marriage-hunters have been significantly reduced."

"We're a committee now?" said Mneme, her eyes brightening at the thought.

"It appears so. Lady Liesl and the other Miss Seabourne are keen to contribute, and Mrs Dr St Swithins is very enthusiastic. Plus, of course, you have the Duchess as your patron."

"A most effective group of ladies," agreed Mneme.

There was a long, thoughtful pause, after which they both began to speak at the same time:

"I don't suppose —"

"If you would care —"

They laughed together, and sipped tea.

"Will you stay with the Duke?" Mneme asked. "Now that he is safely married."

"His Grace's personal protection was only ever a small part of my duties, while he was actively seeking a bride," Mr Thornbury assured her. "His active service to the Queen and the Court of Lords calls upon my professional skills quite often, and when I am not directly needed by the Duke, I have leave to pursue my own interests. I am currently researching a paper on the uses and abuses of sympathetic magic, for example."

"How interesting," she said, meaning it quite genuinely. "So, you will spend a great deal of the year in Town, or at Court?"

"As ever," Mr Thornbury agreed. "But as long as portal travel is exclusive to gentlemen, it is our prerogative as well as our privilege. I would not… expect my future wife, should I marry, to follow me from Isle to Isle because of my profession."

"How thoughtful of you," said Mneme, an edge of cynicism coming into her voice. "And what would this wife of yours do with herself then, while you were so engaged?"

"Why, whatever she wished," said Thornbury. "To follow whatever interests or pursuits she liked, whether that be — quiet solitude, or committees and activism."

"I see." Mneme's cup of tea had gone cold, but she could not bear to stop this exchange to swap it out for a fresh one. She felt on the brink of something exceedingly important. "Where would you live with this theoretical wife of yours?"

"I have the means to buy a property, thanks to the generous support of the Duke," said Mr Thornbury. "I am hesitant to make a final choice on location, however, without knowing whom I am to share the residence with. My own preference would be somewhere quiet, in the country, with a library and a garden."

"A library," said Mneme, her teacup rattling once in her saucer.

"A good-sized library, I think. I have access to the Duke's collection, of course, but a man of research should have his own space to work away from the bustle and chaos." Mr Thornbury smiled again. He should smile all the time. It did quite splendid things to his face. "As should a lady. A library big enough for two sounds most appropriate."

"And when you are busy in Town or at Court or at one of the Duke of Storm's many residences," continued Mneme, "Would you use your privilege of portal travel to ensure you returned home most nights, to share supper with your wife? To discuss your day and your work... and hers... and to build a marriage based on shared interests and companionship?"

"I think," said Mr Thornbury. "That is exactly what I would like." A shadow of concern crossed his face. "Of course, as a man of work, I could never hope..."

"Mr Thornbury," said Mneme. "It may interest you to know that, given the near-scandal that occurred in my family recently, my father has decided that the decision of my future husband should be taken entirely out of my mamma's hands. He is of the belief that I am the best judge as to whom is worthy of my hand."

"That is... remarkably generous of him," said Mr Thornbury, his eyes brightening with what Mneme very much believed to be hope.

"It is important to know what you want in life, and what would make you happy," she said firmly.

"I agree wholeheartedly," said Mr Thornbury. "With that in mind, I believe I have a question to put to you."

Mneme set her teacup on the nearby table, preparing herself. "Before you do, Mr Thornbury, I have a question to put to *you*. Do you think it would be of use to your professional reputation if you had the opportunity to change your name to Seabourne?"

"Why," said Thornbury, taking her hand in his. "It would be a positive boon."

"Well, then," said Mneme, grinning at him. She wondered if she looked as ridiculously happy as he did, here on the lawn surrounded by tables and teacups. "You had better ask your question now. I'm ready."

THE END... for now

A GLOSSARY OF THE TEACUP ISLES

- Bath, Isle of — one of the Teacup Isles: a holiday destination with healing waters
- Bumbleton Palace — a palace in the country
- Continent, the — an extremely large island, beyond the Lyric Sea, foreign but fashionable
- Croquet, the new — a jolly game involving young ladies, sticks, balls and creative sorcery
- Dormouse, Isle of — one of the Teacup Isles: a source of rather good tea
- Gaia — a goddess
- Lyric Sea, the — home to the Teacup Isles
- Manticore, Isle of — one of the Teacup Isles: a lordship
- Memory, Isle of — one of the Teacup isles: quiet, peaceful
- Sandwich, Isle of — one of the Teacup Isles: an earldom
- Season, the — that part of the year when it is warm enough for garden parties, house parties or balls, and unmarried nobility are positively

encouraged to court each other in dramatic fashion
- Shellwich Standing — the Seabourne family home, on the Isle of Memory
- Spellcracker — a professional person whose specialty is the removal, shielding and dissolving of unwanted magics
- Storm, Isle of — one of the Teacup Isles: a dukedom.
- Storm Bolt — the Duke of Storm's townhouse
- Storm North — the Duke of Storm's country seat
- Swan-shaped boats — the only polite manner of travel between islands for those of the female persuasion.
- Sympathetic magic — a minor form of spellcraft, using objects (often charmed) to form small but significant shifts in reality, will or marital status
- Thyme, Isle of — one of the Teacup Isles: featuring the Agnew estate
- Troilish Empire, the — a mysterious and distant land which, nevertheless, values croquet
- Town, Isle of — the centre of most social activity in the Teacup Isles, featuring the Isle of Court
- Uranos — a god
- Wistworia Palace — a palace in Town

ALSO BY TANSY RAYNER ROBERTS

Thanks so much for reading. Please consider leaving a review.

Sign up for my newsletter, Tea and Links (tinyurl.com/tansyrr), for news, special offers and monthly tea reviews, plus a free story!

Mnemosyne Seabourne and Mr Thornbury will return in their next novella: THE FROST FAIR AFFAIR (2020).

Our heroine stumbles across a precarious plot while printing political pamphlets...

Thanks to last Season's scandal involving her family, Miss Mnemosyne Seabourne is officially notorious. Wintering in Town, she hopes to use her new celebrity to campaign about the unfair restriction on portal travel for ladies... while being quietly courted by a certain handsome spellcracker.

As the river freezes over and a spectacular Frost Fair sets up on the ice, Mneme finds herself beset by secret societies, spies and sneaky saboteurs. Who stole her political pamphlets? Who is leaving dead bodies around printing presses for anyone to find?

Mr Thornbury knows more than he's letting on. If she can't trust the man she hoped to marry, Mneme is just going to have to unravel the mystery for herself, quick enough to save both of their lives.

If you enjoy vintage spy adventures, flirtatious couples and cosy sleigh rides, you'll adore this exciting sequel novella to Tea and Sympathetic Magic:

THE FROST FAIR AFFAIR by Tansy Rayner Roberts

I think you'll also enjoy these titles:

UNREAL ALCHEMY (Belladonna U #1)

HOLIDAY BREW (Belladonna U #2)

Light-hearted urban fantasy collections about a geeky student rock band and their friends, attending an Australian university for the magical and unmagical.

THE CREATURE COURT

Intrigue, devastating plot twists and sumptuous detail. Immerse yourself in this dark fantasy trilogy inspired by the 1920s.

Cabaret of Monsters (prequel novella)

Book 1. Power & Majesty

Book 2. The Shattered City

Book 3. Reign of Beasts

CASTLE CHARMING

It's not easy living in a fairy tale kingdom.

Fall in love with the wild, attention-seeking Princes Charming and the poor suckers who work for them. Spinning wheel curses, giant attack beanstalks, fairy invasions and wishes come true. Plus, kissing. So much kissing!

Coming in 2020.

ABOUT THE AUTHOR

Tansy Rayner Roberts is an award-winning Australian science fiction and fantasy author who never wears corsets or muslin. She lives with her family in Tasmania and has been known to pick up the occasional embroidery hoop.

Listen to Tansy on Sheep Might Fly, a podcast where she reads aloud her stories as audio serials.

What tea is Tansy drinking?

Find out at: tinyurl.com/tansyrr when you subscribe to her excellent newsletter.

Follow TansyRR at:
tansyrr.com/
news@tansyrr.com